# FATHER CHRISTMAS

# RAYMOND BRIGGS
# Father Christmas

COWARD-McCANN, INC.
New York

*For my Mother and Father*

*First American Edition 1973*
*Text and illustrations copyright © 1973 by Raymond Briggs*
*All rights reserved*
*ISBN: 0-698-20272-4*
*Library of Congress Catalog Card Number: 73-77885*
*Printed in the United States of America*
*Tenth Impression*

# Father Christmas

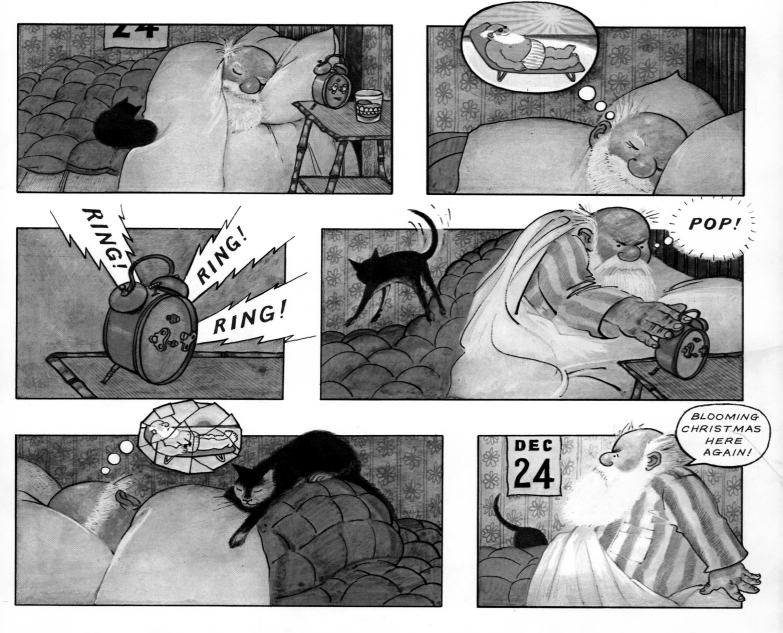

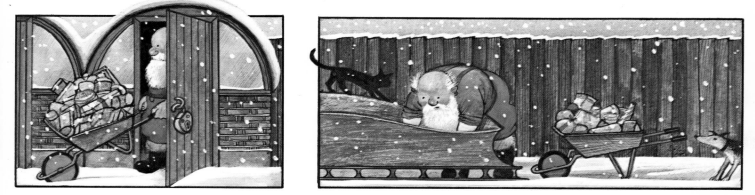

KEEP STILL YOU SILLY DEERS!

EXTENSION

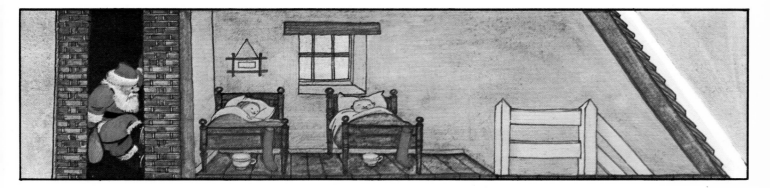

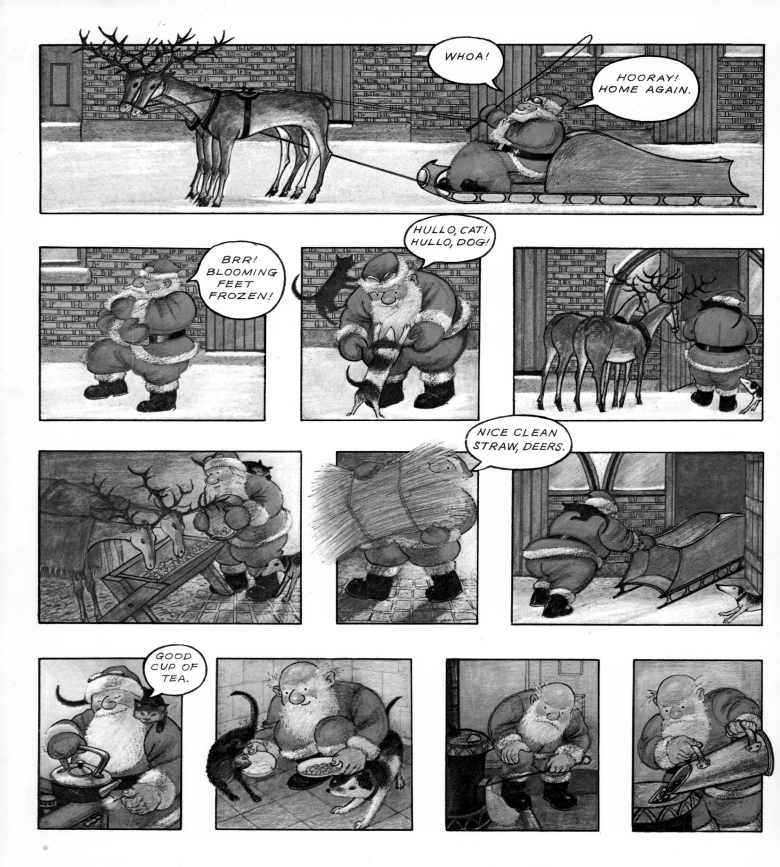

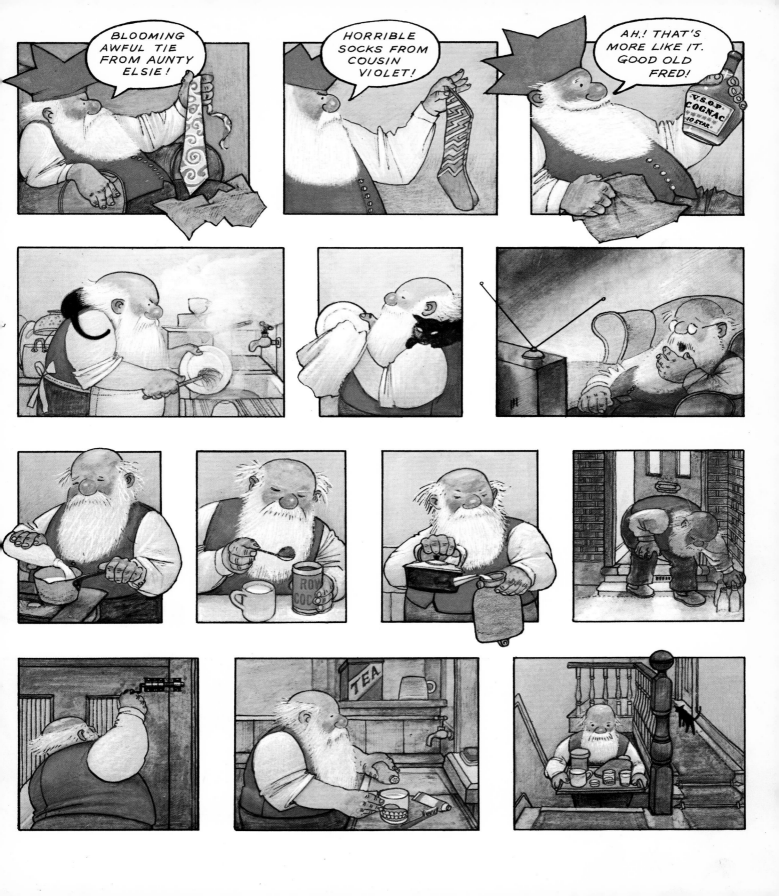

The End